Nathaniel Hall

The Iniquity: A Sermon Preached in the First Church Dorchester

SALZWASSER
VERLAG

Nathaniel Hall

The Iniquity: A Sermon Preached in the First Church Dorchester

Reprint of the original, first published in 1859.

1st Edition 2022 | ISBN: 978-3-37513-278-1

Verlag (Publisher): Salzwasser Verlag GmbH, Zeilweg 44, 60439 Frankfurt, Deutschland
Vertretungsberechtigt (Authorized to represent): E. Roepke, Zeilweg 44, 60439 Frankfurt, Deutschland
Druck (Print): Books on Demand GmbH, In de Tarpen 42, 22848 Norderstedt, Deutschland

THE INIQUITY:

A

SERMON

PREACHED IN

THE FIRST CHURCH. DORCHESTER.

ON SUNDAY, DEC. 11, 1859.

BY NATHANIEL HALL.

BOSTON:

PRINTED BY JOHN WILSON & SON,

22, SCHOOL STREET.

1859.

Rev. NATHANIEL HALL.

DEAR SIR, — We are desirous of having your very acceptable discourses of last Sunday preserved in a permanent form, that they may thereby reach many who have not had an opportunity of hearing them; and we feel sure that we express the wishes of a large number of your parishioners and friends in asking copies of them for publication.

Very respectfully and truly yours,

THOS. C. WALES.
THOMAS GROOM.
WM. E. COFFIN.
WILLIAM POPE, Jr.
FRANKLIN KING.

JNO. H. ROBINSON.
ELISHA T. LORING.
DANIEL DENNY.
FRED. W. G. MAY.
HENRY G. DENNY.

DORCHESTER, Dec. 15, 1859.

GENTLEMEN, —

In deference to your expressed judgment of them, I place the Sermons you request for publication, in your hands, for that purpose, — though written with no such thought.

Very respectfully,

NATHANIEL HALL.

To THOS. C. WALES and others.

SERMON.

Luke x. 27: "THOU SHALT LOVE THY NEIGHBOR AS THYSELF."

John xiii. 34: "A NEW COMMANDMENT I GIVE UNTO YOU, THAT YE LOVE ONE
ANOTHER AS I HAVE LOVED YOU."

FOR reasons which the past week has furnished, I take for my subject, this morning, that always, to so many, distasteful one, — now, to some of you, I fear, more especially so, — the subject of American Slavery.

I am happy in the belief that I possess your confidence in the worthiness of my motive in presenting this subject in the past, so far at least as to lead you to bear with me now, in the persuasion that only a feeling of bounden allegiance to a great and holy cause impels me, and my desire, in the present excited condition of the public mind, the conflict of opinion and feeling among equally wise, and, I doubt not, equally conscientious men, to throw my contribution of light, though it be but a single ray, on the path of duty respecting it. I feel that it is the pulpit's *time* to speak; that, instead of withholding itself because

of this excitement around it, all the more for this
should it speak. It is *always* its time to speak on
this subject. It is a subject bound upon it by
most solemn obligations. And had it, the pulpit
of the Free States, been true to those obligations in
the past; had it not been faithless to the great moral
question of the age in this country; had it not, as
a general 'fact (I say not from what motives; God
knows), had it not practically ignored it, and given
it over to the politician, and to those outside the
church, who have taken it up because the church
would not; had the pulpit lent itself with heart
and might to the antislavery movement, — I believe,
before God, this most unhappy and fearfully threaten-
ing condition of things now upon us would never have
existed. And, in saying this, the assumption is not
that preachers have an especial competency to discuss
the subject, in all its relations; that there is more
wisdom and intelligence in the pulpit for this than in
the hall of legislation, the forum, the editorial chair.
Let it be granted that there is far less. The subject
has other than political and economic relations, which
are likely in the places named to be the only ones
discussed, and not without partisan and unworthy bias.
The subject has relations also to morality and religion, — most intimate, most direct; and, supposing
these relations to get a fair consideration in the
places spoken of, how could it supersede the neces-

sity of the pulpit's discussing them, or excuse its silence upon them? But we well know they do *not* get such discussion there; that these relations are very generally put out of sight, as if they did not exist; or are recognized but to be scoffed at. The preacher should — his calling presumes it of him — see more clearly than other men what the claims of morality and religion are with regard to this question, as to others. Freed by his position from an active participation in the dizzying pursuit of life's meaner good; dealing by profession with absolute and unchanging verities, — he occupies, surely, a vantage-ground above other men for such clearer vision. Should he not tell what he sees? The *theory* of the pulpit is, that it stands amidst the eddying tides and blinding mists of the mortal shores, a lighthouse, flamed by the Eternal Truth, to warn and guide the endangered voyager; to remind and keep him in sight of interests higher than earth's, and more lasting than time's; that it stands a present Christ, a perpetually vocalized Gospel, with its pointings to duty, with its affirmations of the higher law, with its rebukes of sin, alike private and public, no less than with its consoling assurances, its cheering hopes, and heavenly promises.

Will men never choose to discriminate between the treatment of this subject politically and the treatment of it ethically? which latter is all the pulpit claims a right to do. Will they never cease to assume, that, because it has become involved with party politics, it has therefore passed from the province of the religious teacher; and that all treatment of it by him, however strictly on his own ground, is entitled to the epithet of "political preaching"? I undertake to say that there never was a more senseless assumption put forth in all Christendom, — one more to be resisted, if need were, to the very death, — than that the pulpit, standing as the visible exponent of God's truth and law, should have nothing to say in reference to the fact that millions of human beings, in the nation in which it stands, are forcefully deprived of their natural rights, and crushed beneath the heel of a lawless oppression; should have no words of pity for the helpless victims of the wrong, none of rebuke for the authors and abettors of it; that the *pulpit* should have none! — standing in the name of Him whose commandment is, "Thou shalt love thy neighbor as thyself," expanded from its Hebrew limitations into "Love one another as I have loved you," — made thus, as well he called it, "a *new* commandment," alike in the breadth and depth of its meaning.

Consider its meaning, — the breadth of it, — "that ye love one another." The Jew loved his own, — those of his own lineage, people, brotherhood, church. The Gentiles were "dogs:" the Samaritans, though included in the same national boundaries, were hated

and despised. The Jew was not so different in this
from men of other lands and later days. The world
still loves "its own." What barriers do differences
of nationality, caste, condition, color, interpose to the
outflow of our love! Did Christ mean it so? He
has answered that question in the parable of the Samaritan. He has answered it on the cross. Fraternity,
with him, was more than consanguinity. Neighbor-
hood was more than juxtaposition. "The neighbor
was the suffering man, though at the farthest pole."
Humanity he loved. "He died for *all*."

Consider, again, its meaning, — the depth of it, —
"that ye *love* one another." Did he mean by "love"
a barren sentiment, — a feeling whose only fruit is
verbal, unpractical, deedless? Happily, we are not
left to question what he meant. "As I have loved
you" decides it. His love was heartfelt sympathy;
it was helpful service; it was life-giving devotedness.
"He *died* for all."

And now let us take this "new commandment" of
the world's Teacher and Exemplar, at whose tribunal
we all must stand, — are standing now, — by whose
law are judged; this "*new* commandment," and yet
which is but a fulfilling of that thundered from Sinai,
but an illumined transcript of that whispered in the
universal heart; let us take it, and confront with it
the fact before us, — that dark, dread fact, growing
darker and more dreadful with every year and month,

— those millions of the enslaved on our soil to-day, helpless victims of human passion, greed, avarice, lust ; made so, kept so, by a nation's power, and an acquiescent public opinion ; decreed by a nation's judiciary to have " no rights which white men are bound to respect ; " millions, with us in all the attributes of an intellectual, moral, social, religious nature ; for whom, as much as for us, God meant his choicest gifts, and, among them, that which makes so many of his other gifts alone of worth, alone of access, — *freedom ;* for whom, as much as for us, Christ came and died ; whom, as much as us, he loves ; yea, with whom he chose to identify himself, saying, " Inasmuch as ye do it or do it not " (the needed favors in your power to do) " to such as these, ye do it, or not, unto me."

Tell me, can you gather here as Christian believers, can you accept this volume as containing the will and law of Heaven, and say that these have no claim on you for the action, sympathy, consideration, speech, whereby you may possibly serve them ; no claim on you to do whatever you may, consistently with other claims, to lift the yoke of their oppression, to return them their stolen " birthright," — if that can be called *stolen* which they never had, — and allow them to feel the dignity of self-ownership, the dignity, and the incentives, and the privileges, and the chances ? Can you say, in this religious light, in hearing of the Christian call, in sight of the

Christian guide, in hearing of the advent song of
Bethlehem, soon again to be sung in all our churches,
— "good-will to men ;" in sight of the closing act
on Calvary, where good-will to men could no further
go; can you say that the case of these hapless bond-
men is no concern of yours; is not for you to act for,
or consider, or be troubled about?

I know not how it is, kind friends. I do not claim,
God knows, to have a warmer heart than others, or a
truer. I do not believe I have. I see those around
me now to whom I look up, in respect and love, for
their kindliness of heart and generosity of deed, and
yet who do not feel as I do on this subject. I have,
probably, touched no chord within their breasts by
my appeal. There are women, the kindest of mothers, who, when they sing their babes to sleep, and
put their hearts into that "good-night" kiss, and
turn away in the unfearing security that no hand but
God's can take them from their arms, have no thought
for her, who, with heart no less tender than their own
in its maternal instincts, with sensibilities no less
attuned to love's sweet music, stands within the slave-
mart, in the agony that only a mother's heart can
know, and looks for the last time on those whom God
has given her, not because death has taken them, —
she could feel almost happy if that were all, — but
because she must witness their living burial in the pit
of slavery, with not even the satisfaction of knowing

how dark and deep their descent shall be; — takes her parting look; feels, for the last time, their warm breath against her cheek; and then gazes after them, as, with reverted faces and sobbing wail, they go, until sight and hearing have lost their hold of them, and she sinks in a despair which finds no sympathy but with God, no restorative but time.

There are mothers, fathers, who are touched to tears in the knowledge of a bereavement come to others, by death, of a beloved daughter, measuring the sorrow of those parental hearts by what their fond affections tell them would be their own, should she, sitting beside them in the sweet charm of opening womanhood, be taken thus; who are touched by the mere recital of such a loss, though the parties were strangers to them, ay, though the case were known as fiction; and who yet have no tears and no thought for those who see, in the growing beauty which God has stamped on form and feature of their maiden child, but the *signet of her doom,* — a doom darker than death, and against which they cannot lift an opposing finger; they dare not lift a protesting appeal.

There *are* those, we well know, in all our communities, who wilfully shut out the whole subject of slavery from their minds; who will not give it a fair hearing, nor any hearing, if they can help it. There are those, we know, who defend it, — on the ground

of the alleged inherent inferiority of the African race;
of the averred condition of the slave, as physically
comfortable ; of the precedents for slavery which the
Bible furnishes; of the benefits, in point of civiliza-
tion and Christianization, which slavery confers on
its benighted victims. There are these! Let them
be. Of course, the appeal of slavery's victims and
slavery's wrongs would be of no avail with such. It
is of *others* that I ask why it should so greatly be so, in
my utter inability to understand it. The commercial
consideration, I know, is strong, very strong, in and
about our cities; which says "Hush!" — for business'
sake. The prejudice against color is strong, making
the same circumstances less affecting as attaching to
a negro than to a white man. The fear of disunion
is strong; which says, "At all costs, that must be
prevented." Respect for constitutional obligations is
strong; which says, "It is in the *bond* that slavery
shall be tolerated: it should be." The inertia of con-
servatism is strong; which says, "Let alone ; things
will work themselves right: in trying to hasten mat-
ters, you may only make bad worse." The prejudice
against abolitionism is strong, allowing the attention
to be turned aside, by what are called its exaggerations
and fanaticisms, from a fair consideration of the subject. I know all this, and more. But it does not
explain to me the failure, to the extent to which it is
apparently true, of the antislavery appeal. I can un-

derstand that considerations like these should serve to deaden, in some degree, its force; but *not* that, at times, in view of the simple facts on which that appeal is based, the native sentiments of the soul should not heave the superincumbent mass, and flame out and up, forgetful of every thing but justice and mercy.

And I confess that I am forced at times, in view of the public apathy before the facts of slavery's inhumanity and wrong. the seemingly utter obliviousness to the claims of its victims to a consideration and regard, to ask, " Is all humanity gone from us in this direction? Is the milk of human kindness dried up within us? the sentiment of justice paralyzed ? " Where shall we find any marked public recognition — any that is not shamefully inadequate — of the cruelty and crime of slavery, — our own slavery, the pet child of this American republic, — where, away from the abolition platform? Bless God it is *there ;* though more is there which I wish were not. But *this* is there, — an open-mouthed plea for the slave, an open-mouthed condemnation of the wrong that makes him such. And none can tell how broad and deep — broadening and deepening — the influence for right and freedom and humanity which has gone forth from those earnest and devoted men and women.

Not, indeed, that such plea and condemnation are, literally, unheard elsewhere. But from how few among the many pulpits of the land, from how few among its presses, from how few among its public men, is heard a bold, earnest, whole-souled expression of the Christian view and the Christian feeling, — the *humane* view, — in relation to this subject! One might reasonably suppose, that in a community like this, beneath the full blaze of gospel light from its beginnings; with such a history, revolutionary, puritanic, — its souls would be all aflame at the near presence, within the confederacy of which it forms a part, of four millions of human beings bound in the most abject form of bondage the world has known. How sadly far from it! I looked in vain in the applauded speech of a distinguished individual in Faneuil Hall, on Thursday last (I name it as an indication, and not as a personality), for the slightest evidence of a single heart-throb for the slave, of a single throe of righteous indignation at the crime of slavery. There were eloquent invocations of sympathy for the imperilled slave-owner, — imperilled as a consequence of a Heaven-defying sin against humanity; but none, no word of sympathy, no verbal remembrance, of those millions so *sinned against.* There were most earnest deprecations of bloodshed by servile insurrection ; but no allusion to the blood daily shed by the wearing, wasting over-toil in cane-field and rice-swamp. None, of course, would object to the invocation of sympathy for the South. God knows,

as itself knows, how large its claim for it. They are
our brethren there, our "neighbors." We are to
show them the love both of sympathy and of service;
but *not*, I protest, *not* to the forgetfulness of the
victims of their oppression. *They* are no less our brethren, no less our neighbors; *more* entitled to our
sympathy and service for their very ignorance and
weakness and long-endured abuses. Which would
Christ, think you, have soonest remembered? We
should sympathize with the South; but as we do
with those who are reaping the natural and inevitable
fruits of their transgression. It has sown the wind to
reap the whirlwind. It has seeded its soil with violence; and what but violence, unless hindered by a
repentant righteousness, can spring upon it? Are
the laws of the moral universe abrogated or sus-
pended in favor of this republic? We should sympathize with the South; not, indeed, in Pharasaic
assumption, as if we were the unsinning and the true,
— God forbid! our own self-convicted hearts forbid!
— but as those who verily are not guiltless of our bro-
thers' blood, in so far as, by act or influence, wilfully
or thoughtlessly, individually or collectively, we may
have aided or consented to the inhumanity and the
wrong; as those who are sharing, and are yet to
share more largely, of its bitter fruits; and who are
ready, in the spirit of a fraternal good-will, to unite
in any effort, which conscience can approve, for its

abolishment. But let us not mock the Eternal Justice by consenting to palter with it, to palliate it; to be, for friendship's sake, or interest's sake, or safety's sake, any longer, however indirectly, its willing and unprotesting upholders. The chief ground of fear for the North at this juncture — what is it? That by its honest-hearted sympathy with an heroic man, who, in the name of God, assailed their institution, it may provoke the South to disunion? Is it not rather, far rather, that for the sake of the Union, in self-interest or timidity, it will consent to farther concessions of its principles and its manhood; increasing thus, how surely, the real evil; debauching yet more the public conscience; delaying a reckoning which must needs come, only to make it the more overwhelming at last?

The word, I feel, which God is speaking to the slaveholders of this land and their abettors, through that most remarkable event which has so startled them, from that scaffold in whose blood they seek in vain to stifle their alarm, — that word is "Repent, reform." And that word — as God's, not its own; not in arrogancy, not in passion — should the North take up, as the burden and spirit of its appeal. It is the kind word, the friendly word, the saving word. But, heeded or unheeded by the South, with the North should be the unalterable decision, We will no longer be partners in the upholding and cherishing of this accursed barbarism. We will no longer be tied up to a complicity in this intolerable outrage and affront to Christianity and the age.

Let us remember, friends, that this impersonality, "the North," is composed of individuals; that we are among them; that, as such, we have duties in relation to this matter of slavery, which it becomes us religiously to fulfil. And, first, we should acquaint ourselves — it is the bounden duty of every one of us, man and woman — with the facts of slavery, to the extent practicable. How many never read a publication, never hear a lecture, touching this subject! They are without the true feeling about it, because without knowledge. We should cherish the feeling which knowledge would beget, not morbidly, not fanatically, but in natural, healthy, Christ-like sympathies for the wronged, and in holy detestation of the wrong. It is the very spirit of God. Quench it not. We should give action to the heart's promptings in doing whatever and all we may, in and through the spirit of Christ, for slavery's downfall and extinction. And, withal, we should give ourselves to prayer, — for the oppressed, for the oppressor, for light, strength, compassion, patience, as our own need with regard to them; the prayer of faith and trust in Him, who, amid clouds and darkness, has justice and judgment as the habitation of his throne; all whose attributes are one in their opposition to oppression; and who,

sooner or later, will show himself to have been on
the side of truth and freedom and right, in the ever-
waging conflict of these with falsehood and despotism
and iniquity.

The work is God's. We can be but his instruments: we *can* be such. "Wherefore, put on the
whole armor of God, that ye may be able to stand in
the evil day, and, having done all, to stand."

THE MAN, — THE DEED, — THE EVENT:

A

SERMON

PREACHED IN

THE FIRST CHURCH, DORCHESTER

ON SUNDAY, DEC. 4, AND REPEATED DEC. 11, 1859.

BY NATHANIEL HALL.

BOSTON:
PRINTED BY JOHN WILSON AND SON,
22, SCHOOL STREET.
1859.

SERMON.

John xi. 50: "It is expedient for us that one man should die for the people."

THE American Pulpit can have but one theme to-day. To decline, for any other, that given in the public tragedy whose shadow is yet upon us, would be to turn away from the very call of God, as heard in his providence, — heard in the awakened minds and quickened sensibilities of a people. So, at least, do I feel it, and must do accordingly. I have forborne to speak hitherto of the affair thus consummated, not because it has not had for me an absorbing interest, but because I wished to wait until that consummation should have passed, until it should wear its death-crown, and be given over in its wholeness, as now it is, to the keeping of history. I have forborne too, let me add, because I have stood in awe — as I do still — before an event so full of significance, so full of teaching, so full of God, lest I might not interpret it aright; lest in a human weakness, through sympathy with the cause in whose interest it befell, I might be led to see in it more, or beneath the influence of contagious opinion, in a human weakness still, which suffers others' judgments to becloud the moral vision, I might see less, than in truth was there. I would simply see what is there, and tell what I see.

On Friday last, the 2d of December, a man, ac-. cused and convicted of capital offences against the laws of Virginia, was publicly executed therefor under those laws. What is there here to quicken the pulses of a nation? What is there in this, that the eyes of twenty millions of people should have been turned, on that day, to that scaffold, — some in tearful sympathy, some in exulting scorn, some in depressing fears, but all with a commanding *interest;* an interest which, for weeks before, had waited, as for nothing else, for the words spoken in his imprisonment, as the million-voiced press reported them, in every dwelling in the land? What is there in this, that the sudden death-knell of the patriarch-prince of American letters, laurelled with the purest admiration of three generations, should have been comparatively unnoticed, in anticipation of that of this sentenced felon? Let us expand that statement of the occurrence by its interconnected facts, and we shall see.

A man of threescore years, of New-England birth, of Puritan descent, and marked in youth and manhood

by the characteristic virtues of that noble stock; a man
nurtured upon the Bible; a man of prayer; a man in
whom the religious element was the ruling and inciting one; a man, the uncompromising sternness of
whose integrity was in union with a childlike sim-
plicity and a self-denying benevolence, — this man,
for following out the impulse of that benevolence, in
a certain way, towards a certain class; for putting his
religion into forceful deeds; for obeying the inward
call, as doubly heard in conscience and in heart; for
seeking to give freedom to an outcast race, whose
oppressions he had borne, through a score of years, as
if they were his own; for "remembering," in the only
way that seemed to him effective, — in the way, as he
felt, which Heaven ordered him, — "them that are
in bonds, as bound with them;" for striking a sacri-
legious blow at the Dagon of a nation's worship,
whereto government, society, religion, commerce, law,
obsequiously bow down, — *this man*, *for this*, on
the day and place aforesaid, was hung as a malefac-
tor; and hence, in these added facts of the case,
hence essentially, that wide-spread interest and deep
sensation the event produced. It was the man, it was
the motive, it was the object; it was the deed, not in
itself, but in its revelations; in its results manifest,
and those, far more, of which it is the prophecy and
the harbinger, at once the seed and the germinating
influence.

4

The man and the event, — they offer themselves as distinct sources of instruction and impression. There are differences of opinion respecting the man; though only, I believe, — which is most remarkable, — in this particular manifestation of himself. But, let these differences be what they may, while they will affect the moral teaching of their related point, — the man in his deed, — making it more or less, or not at all, impressive, it need not affect, in the least, the lessons from the *event*, — the event as such, and in its attendant revelations and practical suggestiveness.

First, the man and the deed; the man *in* his deed. I see in him — as may already have been inferred — an heroic nobleness; a moral intrepidity; an unflinching conscientiousness; a religious self-devotion; a resolute pursuance, for years, of a purpose to which his soul was wedded by holiest ties; which he had espoused, before Heaven, as divine; had sworn to be faithful to, through all hazards, at any cost, unto death; and for which, at last, in a lofty disregard of personal consequences, in an unquestioning confidence in a righteous God, he hazarded and gave his life. It is the *motive* stamps the deed; it is the *purpose* makes the man, morally regarded. Call him, if you will, mistaken, foolish, — mistaken as to the justifiableness of the means employed, foolish in his estimate of the efficiency of those means in relation to his end. What has it to do with the moral rightness and wisdom of

the man? If you deny him the attribute of a pru-
dential rationality, you must accord him the virtues,
in glorious measure, of courage, magnanimity, hu-
maneness, truth. If you deny him a perfect appre-
hension of the Christian law, you must accord to him
a whole-souled allegiance to what he *did* apprehend
as such. If you call him, in disparagement, an *Old-
Testament* Christian, you must allow him to have
been *that:* ay, and more than that he was; combin-
ing with a holy valor a philanthropy, which, in the
choice of its objects and the disinterestedness of its
aim, only Christianity could inspire. If you say he
believed in a " God of battles," he believed, at any rate,
in a God who battled for *right* as against wrong, for
the *oppressed* as against the oppressor, and who puts
swords into his servants' hands, to do, if need be,
likewise.

This, at least, we *know* of John Brown, — that he
allied himself, head and heart and hand, with the
legally oppressed class in this country; that he saw,
that he felt, as if they were his own, the wrongs they
suffer, and gave his all, himself, for their deliverance.
Whatever we may deny about him, of whatever we
may be doubtful, *so much* we *know.* His veracity is
unimpeachable; even his enemies confess, and stood
in awe before it; and this *he* asserts of himself. His
wife also, widow now, of noble worth, testifies to this
feeling and purpose as among the deepest and dearest

of his heart. " He has borne," she says, "the yoke of
the oppressed, as if upon his neck, for thirty years."
Every thing known of him, every thing said of him,
by reliable witnesses ; his whole past ; the interval,
above all, of his imprisonment, and his sublimely-met
end, — all force us to the belief, that in the spirit of a
compassionating benevolence, joined with a fervid love
of justice and of right, he had made it, by prayer and
vow, the one leading object of his life, to emancipate, as
best he might, the enslaved.   Nor is there any thing
to show that personal motives of any sort, of a
character sordid or ambitious or revengeful, mingled
at all with the highest — no, not even the *latter* —
marvellous height of moral attainment, in view of
his own heart-rending experience of the bereaving
cruelties of the slave-power. *See him thus*, in this
light alone, as one who, in the consciousness of a
righteous cause, and in pity for an outcast and despised race, in a sublime recklessness opposed himself
to a nation's prostituted power, — a recklessness which
had in it, it may be, a higher wisdom, a truer sanity,
seen from its providential point, than we yet can
know ; — see him thus, and how can we but honor
him ? If we honor those in all the ages who have
dared and died for the oppressed ; if we honor the
martyrs for liberty on our own soil ; nay, I speak it
reverently, if we honor Christ, who identified himself
with the poor and forsaken, and calls upon his follow-

ers to do so, in sacrificing service, — how can we but
honor the memory of this executed man? See the
man in his motive, and tell me why. Separate the
circumstances which involve not the moral character
of his enterprise from those which express it, and tell
me why. God save us from that inability to discriminate between the mere form, providential or mistaken,
of the manifestation of a principle, and its essential
being and activity; from that prejudiced and per-
verted vision, which shall let any of his true heroes
pass unmarked by us as such, whether in public or
private life, seated in power or dangling from a gal-
lows, crowned with success or crushed by failure!
For myself, I rejoice that He has raised up such a
one in the person of this humble man. I rejoice that
He has startled a nation, given to selfish toils and
demeaning indulgences and base expediences, by the
unwonted apparition of a *man ;* a man heroically earnest for righteousness' sake ; a man daring to follow
a principle, wheresoever it may lead ; to put his religion into act, and take the consequences, though one
be death. Some call this fanaticism ; some call it
madness. Would to God there were more of it in the
world, call it what they may ; more vital faith in
principles, in God, in a God of righteousness, a present God, a helping God ; a faith that would keep
men from everlastingly calculating the probable and
the expedient, as if there was no Being wiser and

stronger than they; as if right was not always the expedient, to abide by it the only success!

I hope to be understood, as one speaking on this subject is very likely not to be. I have spoken approvingly of the principles and motives of the man, as apart from the course he was led by these to adopt. That that course had the approval of his own conscience, that it seemed right to him, there can be no doubt; and while, in our judgment of it, we are allegiant to our truer view, as we deem it, of the Christian law, let us not do his memory the injustice to ascribe to him what he did not design. How does it appear, though so generally assumed, that he designed to employ force, aggressively and destructively, in the accomplishment of his purpose, or to incite the slaves to insurrection? On the contrary, he says of himself, in his speech before the court, — this man whose word was truth,—"I never did intend murder or treason, or the destruction of property, or to incite slaves to rebellion, or to make insurrection: I never encouraged men to do so, but always discouraged any idea of the kind." He had given freedom to slaves elsewhere, "without," as he says, "the snap of a gun." He meant to do it here on a larger scale, but, if possible, at the same bloodless cost; though, I confess, it seems to me the fanaticism of credulity to suppose it could be so. He would have confronted with his mustering forces, Moses-like, this later Pharaoh, with a "Thus saith the Lord, Let my people go;" an unresisting obedience to which mandate would doubtless, so far as *he* was concerned, have been followed by a peaceable retreat. That he would have employed or countenanced force, in recklessness or revenge, for aught but self-defence in humanity's cause, is, as the man has shown himself to us, a moral impossibility.

I believe in truth and love as the overcoming power of moral evil. I would not compromise my adhesion to this, as eminently the Christian rule, through my admiration of those, who, though from highest motives, for noblest ends, make use of aggressive force. But let us be consistent, and not condemn it in John Brown at Virginia, while we applaud it, as employed by great historic names, in other lands and our own, for ends no more worthy, that lifted to Heaven a far *less* beseeching appeal. Is it *success* gives merit to undertakings for human freedom? or the *theatre* whereon enacted? or the *race* in whose behalf? And let those, who are so ready to make use of Christ's teaching as ground for condemnation in the instance before us, remember that his precept of non-resistance is not his only one; that he had something to say about *love and duty to one's neighbor;* that he commended especially to our imitation him who found his "neighbor" in the man who had "*fallen among thieves,*" and staid to bless him, though priest and Levite passed.

I pass from the man and the deed to the event, as
a distinct source of instruction and impression.

And, first, it yields new and more convincing proofs
of the diabolicalness of that " institution," which de-
mands, in order to its safety, its existence, the death
of the bravely true, the morally heroic ; which dares
not pardon such, dares not imprison merely, dares
not delay the fatal end, but must straightway kill:
or, to put it in another form, that system which de-
mands for its support laws against which the natural
conscience, the religious sense, rebels ; which makes
that treason which God makes duty, and counts
those felons whom the universal heart calls heroes.
Here is a man distinguished for his moral nobility,
his love of truth, honor, justice, benevolence, — for
his unshrinking fealty to these, — and Virginia hangs
him. " He broke her laws." Yes, but only because
the law of Eternal Justice was broken in their enact-
ment; because they stood between prostrate millions
and the uplifting boon and birthright which the God
within him yearned to give them. *Slavery* hung him.
Of course it would. It can do nothing better with a
true man, for its own interest's sake. What a condition of things has this affair caused a revelation
of in the Slaveholding States! What a condition of
things to exist in one-half of a Christian republic!
Such fears of truth ; such suppression of honest
speech ; where peace and safety can only be secured

by stifling — ay, below a whisper — the noblest sentiments of the soul ; where the Bible is regarded, and
dealt with, as offensively incendiary, and can only be
tolerated by covering up its golden rule, its parable
of the good Samaritan, and its other humanities !
What a state of society, when a score of men, enter-
ing it at its borders, and asserting God's claim upon
his stolen children, and going to work to enforce it,
cause a panic of terror through an entire population,
which every light upon the horizon, the most insig-
nificant occurrence, renews and heightens, — a terror
for what *they* may do, who, we are told, are so con-
tented and happy, and gratefully attached ! Truly,
one may well divide his pity between the slaveholder
and the slave.

Again : the event gives new and startling proof of
the instability of the social system built on slavery,
— of slavery itself as an instituted power. Above
what volcanic possibilities is the South seen to stand,
— does *it* see itself to stand, — which may flame at
any moment into dire realities ; the igniting sparks of
truth flying in all the winds of heaven without, and
vainly striven against lest they should light within !
The danger most fearful to the South, and most
imminent, is not from abroad. Left to itself, — so
far as the all-pervading spirit of the age *can* leave it,
so far as any direct interference is concerned, —
it is left with its worst enemy, in the elements self-

engendered in its own bosom. What may not be, when once those fettered millions know their might; when they know, as this event will help them to, the fact of an existing sympathy for them beyond their borders, but only just beyond, may be within, — a sympathy willing to peril life for their deliverance? What may not be, when that other element of danger (the non-slaveholders), seething in secret, none may know how hotly, — for it has no organ of expression to the world nor to itself, — when *this* element shall find vent in voice and deed, and know and use its now arrogantly despised power? It is idle to deny the fact of this insecurity and peril. It is seen by this occurrence as it had not been before. And was it not to be looked for, in the very nature of things, by the very ordinance of the Almighty? A system, social or civil, founded in injustice, — must it not bear within it the elements of rottenness and evil? Well may it be that the event under consideration has drawn attention anew to so grave a fact, has furnished new testimony to it; well for the South, — God grant it! — in its insane clinging to slavery as a good; well for the North, in its wicked complicity and irresolute paltering with so great a wrong.

Again: this event has shown the South, what it has seemed unable to conceive, that the opposition to slavery at the North is not the offspring of sectional hate or sentimental heat, of self-interest or passion,

but of a constraining principle, of a religiously-felt
obligation. John Brown represents to them and to
the world, in the inciting and pervading motive of his
enterprise, the true grounds of that opposition, deep
and abiding as the principles of rectitude and mercy.
He had nothing to gain by it of an earthly sort, if he
succeeded; every thing to lose, if he failed. There
was no feeling of retaliation or revenge to be grati-
fied. He was willing to sacrifice his all for those of
whom he knew no more than that they were enslaved,
towards whom he had no other relation than the
human, whose claim on him was that alone of suffering and helplessness. The antislavery reform is a
moral and religious one. The abolitionists have
stood, from the beginning, — and it is this which has
given a moral dignity and glory to their enterprise,
lifting it far above all political movements, — they
have stood on the essential and eternal right, and
based their appeals on that to the conscience and the
heart. Hence their success. Hence, whatever they
have gained they have gained for ever. There is,
there can be, no ebb to the on-sweeping tide of antislavery sentiment. How preposterous to think to
stay it by politic deprecations, to think to bind it by
constitutional compacts and judicial decisions! I
tell you they shall be as stubble before its majestic
swell.

Again: the event yields new illustration of the

vast superiority, in potential influence, of deeds to words. There have been torrents of speech — declamation, argument, persuasion, invective — levelled for years, in the Free States, against the slave-power. Nor has it been in vain. It was needed. It has wrought incalculable good. But here is one so terribly in earnest, so meaning what he says, that he *must act*; that, throwing himself unreservedly upon his principles, he *does* act; and does thus, whatever he fails to do, a work for freedom — so it would seem, viewed in its higher bearings — which years of words alone had failed to do. The lesson is not that such like deeds are to be repeated, or are in themselves right. By no means. But *this*, that *deeds*, *some* deeds, such as our avowed principles authorize and demand of us, should back our words, should prove our earnestness, would we be efficient instruments against the instituted iniquity of our land. This faithful servant of God put his life-swaying idea and feeling into that embodiment which seemed to and for him worthy and right and best; and has gained by it a success different from, but far beyond, all that he proposed to himself or hoped for. Obedience to a conviction, — self-sacrificing, *life*-sacrificing obedience, — it can shake even the citadel of American Slavery. *Life*-sacrificing, I say. What a power there is in blood, freely given and poured forth for a righteous end! They little knew, who heard it, the profound significance, prophetically hidden, of that saying uttered in the Jewish Sanhedrim, with reference to him, the divine Emancipator, at whom it so blindly aimed, — " It is expedient for us that one man die for the people, and that the whole nation perish not." *We* little know what sacred expediency may be yet shown to be involved in this recent dying; how much it may do, in the workings of a spiritual Providence, to save a nation's perishing.

Friends, who can doubt that a crisis is approaching in the conflict, truly called " irrepressible," between freedom and slavery, in our country? Let us feel that we each have an influence—however small, not unimportant—in the great decision ; and let us employ it, as God may give the opportunities, in the true spirit of his Christ, for freedom, humanity, himself; putting a cheerful and untrembling faith in the overruling and righteous Providence.

> " All is best; though we oft doubt
> What the unsearchable dispose
> Of highest Wisdom brings about,
> And ever best found in the close.
> Oft he seems to hide his face,
> But unexpectedly returns,
> And to his faithful champions, soon or late,
> Bears witness gloriously."